City Cop

City
Cop

FRED J. COOK

Doubleday & Company, Inc.
Garden City, N.Y.

Library of Congress Catalog Card Number 78–60284
ISBN: 0-385-13460-6
Copyright © 1979 by Doubleday & Company, Inc.

Preface

His name is Carlos Acha. He is a young Puerto Rican, about five feet ten inches tall, with a strong, compact body. His eyes are so dark they look almost black, and he has a wide-lipped, good-humored smile.

Carlos Acha is a New York City policeman.

From the time he was a boy, growing up in a tough West Side section of New York, he had just one goal: to wear the uniform.

"In those days, back in the early sixties," Carlos says, "there were only two classes of people I knew who got any respect: the teachers and the cops. I wanted that respect."

For Carlos, it wasn't easy. When he first came to New York, as a boy of seven, he couldn't speak a word of English. He learned. He worked hard at it. It took years of effort—and service with the U. S. Marines in Vietnam—before he was appointed to the force, in May 1973.

Since then, he has seen it all. He has served in one of the toughest precincts of New York. The shields of seven slain policemen hang on the wall as a reminder of just how tough and dangerous it is. Carlos knew two of those slain cops well.

On patrol in the very section in which they were killed, Carlos has dealt with junkies, rioters, burglars, psychos. He has been twice injured and hospitalized. Despite the dangers, he likes his job.

He is proud to be what he is—a New York City cop. This is his story as he told it to me.

City Cop

1

Growing Up

I had a hard time at first. In Puerto Rico, my father had sent me to a private school when I was two years old. By the time I was 7, I had been promoted to the fifth grade.

Then my father sent me to New York to join my mother, Maria Acha Espada. We are a very well-guarded family. Espada means sword, and Acha means ax.

My mother had come to New York the previous year. It was pretty hard to feed a family of five in Puerto Rico in those days, and my mother, grandmother, and two sisters had come here.

They had an apartment on Ninety-third Street between West End Avenue and Riverside Drive. It was a very tough neighborhood, running with street gangs. These were all made up of older boys, in their teens, and fortunately for me, I was too young to get involved with them.

My greatest problem was that I couldn't understand a word of English. I didn't know whether someone was talking about eggs or meat. So, naturally, when I went to school, I was knocked back to the third grade. It was a great shock to me—and to my father, too—because I had been considered bright in school in Puerto Rico. But here the language barrier really set me back.

I guess the first words you learn in any language are the dirty ones, and for a time I was getting my mouth washed out with soap pretty often. Even after I began to learn some English, certain words gave me trouble for a long time. "Ask" would come out "hask," and "eggs" would come out "heggs." I kept wanting to put that "h" on everything.

From the time I entered high school, my one

ambition was to be a cop. There was the appeal of the uniform. All kids are fascinated by a uniform. And in those days—it may seem funny now—the two classes of people you really looked up to and respected were the teachers and the cops.

Sometimes people ask me whether I didn't think about the dangers of the life, about the possibility of getting shot and killed. All I can say is that I never worried about that. You can walk out your door and get hit on the head by a piece of falling concrete. You can get mugged and killed, or run down by a truck in the street. Anything can happen to you in life, and there is no sense worrying about it.

When I first thought about becoming a policeman, I was encouraged by a special trainee program the city started around the end of 1964. Under this program, when you were eighteen you had the chance to become an aide around a police station. That meant working in the record files and performing minor chores. But it gave you a foot in the door, and when you were twenty-one, you could be sworn in on the force.

The program showed me the possibilities, but it didn't help me much at the time. The Vietnam War was raging at its worst when I graduated from high school. I knew I would soon be drafted by the Army. So I decided to enlist in the U. S. Marines before I was called up.

The marine training then was *real* training. If you didn't have muscles, they would give you some. If you had hair, they would take it away. It wasn't like it is today, when a mother can cause trouble by complaining to her congressman about how badly her little boy is being treated. Then, if you needed to be knocked on your rear end, you got knocked on your rear end. There were no ifs about it. By the time you came out of basic training, you had developed muscles you never knew you had.

My unit shipped out to Vietnam in early 1968. We arrived only a short time after the Communists' surprise Tet offensive had threatened to overrun the country and capture the capital city of Saigon. My outfit was sent up to the front line to relieve the battalion that had been hit hardest during the attack. But I wasn't at the front long. I had been promoted to staff sergeant, and I was sent back to Chu-lai, where I had a job that involved handling liquid oxygen and liquid nitrogen for the hospitals and the Air Force.

After four years' service with the Marine Corps, I came back to New York in May 1969. I still wanted to be a cop, and I took the written exam for the Police Department. In August, I was notified that I had passed, and I was called in for the physical test. This consisted of jumping hurdles, running, broad jumping, doing push-ups and pull-ups, and lifting weights. With the muscles the Marines had given me, this drill presented no problem. I was told I would be called up soon.

But then came the job freeze. The city was getting into bad financial trouble, and no more policemen were being hired. It was very discouraging. Here I had waited all those years. I had wanted just one thing: to get on the force. I had had it practically made. And then the door was slammed in my face.

I suppose I could have given up, but I didn't. I wanted to be a policeman so bad that nothing else would satisfy me. I knew that I was high on the list of those to be hired if the city's finances improved. So I marked time, working at any job I could find.

Since I am a good swimmer, I had had a job as a lifeguard with the Department of Parks when I was in high school. I got that job back for the summertime. In the winter, I worked for an oil company in the Bronx. Between the two jobs, I made a living—and waited. I waited for four long years, before Mayor John Lindsay decided, in January 1973, that he had to have more cops on the streets. I was hired on May 29, 1973.

Once you join the Department, you are sent to the Police Academy for training. My class was the first at the Academy to have more women than men in it. The city had just begun to train women for street patrol, and our class had 125 women and 90 men. We were divided into five companies. Since I had been a staff sergeant in the Marines, I was made a platoon sergeant in charge of one of the companies.

I was lucky. In my company there was a pretty blonde with sparkling blue eyes and a quick, lively manner. I soon discovered that she was as smart as she was beautiful, a rare combination, and we began to see a lot of each other. That's the way I met Dina, who is now my wife.

The Police Academy training program is a good one. You are kept busy for five and a half months learning everything you will have to know to become a good police officer. Your days are divided into four hours of classroom work in the morning, a lunch-hour break, then three hours downstairs in the gym. You are prepared mentally and physically for the street.

The training includes a complete study of the penal laws and police science. You are taught how to issue summonses, how to handle neighborhood disputes, how to deal with everything from a stolen car to a bank robbery.

Then you are drilled for two or three weeks on how to handle a gun. You're rated on the firing range on the basis of fifty rounds, each round counting two points. To make expert, you have to have a perfect score, 100; 90–99 is sharpshooter; 75–89, marksman. I always shot about 98 or 99; I could never make 100. I'm right-handed, but you have to learn to shoot with both hands. Every two rounds out of fifty, I had to shoot with my left hand, and that left hand always gave me trouble. I was a sharpshooter, but I could never make expert.

Our training lasted from May to the end of October 1973. Then we were graduated from the Academy. Dina and I were both assigned for

7

field training to the Midtown South district. This was in the heart of the city, where a lot of large department stores are. There we began to learn the difference between the classroom and the street.

2

The First Arrest

I think every cop will always remember the details of his first arrest. Mine didn't amount to much, but it was an eye opener as to the way the system works.

Once you have graduated from the Police Academy, you are not just put out on the street on your own. Each rookie is assigned a veteran officer to guide and teach him. These officers are known as "field training officers," and your field training officer goes with you on your beat for eight weeks. He teaches you how to act in certain situations. He watches everything you do and grades you, because you are on probation for one full year.

You soon learn that what may have seemed simple in the classroom isn't so simple in the real life of the street. At the Academy, for instance, they might throw on the screen a problem like this: John Doe has just had his car stolen. Instructions are flashed on the screen to tell you just what procedures you should take: how to get John Doe's name, his address, the registration number of his car; how to report the incident. It all seems so simple.

But you soon find out that it isn't. On the street, you're faced with a man who is practically beside himself with anger because someone has just stolen his car. He's jumping up and down, demanding that you do something about it. Right away, too.

So the first thing you have to do is to try to calm him down enough so that you can make some sense out of what he is saying. But he doesn't want to calm down and relax. He wants his car, and he may even get mean about it. Your field training officer, of course, has dealt with cases like this many times. He helps you to get through to the car owner, to calm him down and get the information you need. Only then can you even begin to fill out the papers that must be filed in each case.

A rookie cop is much like a young bird that is just beginning to learn to fly. Like the bird, you hang around with your mother—your field training officer—for eight weeks. Then you have to fly on your own.

My first arrest was made during this eight-week period when my field training officer was teaching me the ropes. We were on patrol near the entrance of the B. Altman & Co. department store, at Fifth Avenue and Thirty-fourth Street, when an elderly woman came running out screaming, "They've just stolen my pocketbook!"

She was pointing to three youths between sixteen and twenty who had run down the street and were just jumping into a taxicab. My field training officer raced around to get on one side of the cab, and I drew my gun and ran to the near side.

"I'm a police officer. Don't move," I shouted as I yanked open the front door of the cab.

The cabbie was so scared he scrambled right out the door on the other side. As he did, I saw one of the youths throw the woman's pocketbook into the street, trying to get rid of the evidence. But I caught him in the act and collared all three of them.

Then the trouble began—and my education along with it.

We took the three of them to court. Of course, the elderly woman had to go along with us as the complaining witness. I soon began to feel sorry for her. The way our judicial system works, the courts are so jammed that you can't just go in with a simple case like this and get it quickly taken care of.

In this instance, we waited from five o'clock in the afternoon until two o'clock the next morning. Still the old lady's purse-snatching case hadn't been called. Finally, she signed a report describing what had happened, and they let her go home.

By the time the three youths finally came before the judge, it was getting so late that he put them on probation and told them to appear later. But, of course, they never did.

The judge then issued a warrant for their arrest, but nothing ever happened. They never showed. I was called down to court four more times on this case. I would be in court at ten o'clock in the morning, and the clerk would call out the names of the defendants and "Police Officer Acha." I would stand up to answer the call. But no one else stood up.

"All right, Officer Acha," the clerk would say, "just wait for a while and we'll call the case again."

I would wait until 11:30 A.M., when the clerk would again call out the names of the defendants and "Police Officer Acha." I would stand up. I would be the only one standing. Finally, I would be told to go back to my station house.

I was in court five times on that case, the first time the day I made the arrest and then four times after that when the kids were supposed to show. But they never did, and nothing ever happened to them.

Every time I was called down to court, I wasted a couple of hours or more. I could have been out on the street doing the job I'm hired to do. That is why I say this first arrest was an education for me. I learned that the court system is either so tied up or so easy to get through without punishment that this kind of thing goes on all the time in all types of cases. And, of course, the young hoods on the street know that this is the way it works, and they take advantage of it.

Friends sometimes ask me what can be done to straighten things out. I doubt if they will ever get straightened out. The problems are just too great.

We don't have the means to handle what we have to handle; that's number one. During the city-wide electrical blackout in July 1977, thousands of persons took to the streets, smashing windows, looting stores, making off with hundreds of thousands of dollars' worth of goods of all kinds. I had been doing my two weeks' training with the Marine Corps Reserves at the time, so I wasn't there.

But when I came back, I found the Department had arrested some three thousand looters, though only about one thousand cases were ever processed. Under the Constitution, everyone who is accused of a crime has the right to a hearing within forty-eight hours. There was just no way the courts could handle three thousand cases in forty-eight hours. So most of the looters went scot free. Those who had rioted and looted and ruined a small businessman's chance to make a living were back on the streets in no time. A few received slap-on-the-wrist penalties, but little more than that, for one simple reason: there aren't jails enough to hold them all.

It's frustrating. Those of us on the force have, at least, the satisfaction of knowing we did our job. We did the best we could. We feel sorry for the victims of this type of crime. The victims, however, often don't realize that. Understandably, they are bitter. They have a grudge and sometimes they take it out on us, because we're out there in uniform where everyone can see us.

We try to explain: "Man, we did our job. We arrested them and took them to court. After that, it's out of our hands. It's up to the courts."

That's something that's hard for most citizens to understand: the difference between the jobs of the cops and the courts. They just figure, "Well, the cops should take care of it." They don't see that we can go only so far, we can do only so much. We get the blame for things we can't help.

3

The Ninth

I never knew crime could be so bad until I was transferred to the Ninth Precinct, on the Lower East Side of Manhattan. What I found there was a shock and an eye opener to me. The Ninth covers a fourteen-block square, but those few blocks are so crime-ridden they deserve to be called Hell's Kitchen.

Every type of crime you can think of is there. There are prostitutes, male prostitutes, junkies, bums, burglars, muggers, killers. The kids start a life of crime at seven or eight years of age—and go on from there.

The reason that I was transferred to the Ninth was that Dina and I got married. There is a rule in the Department that married couples can't serve in the same precinct.

Dina and I had been going together for about seven months—her name was Beraldine Leli before we were married—and we decided to have Judge Bruce Wright marry us. He was a very tough black judge and one of Dina's instructors at the John Jay College for Criminal Justice. We just walked into his court one day while he was holding a criminal trial, and he called a recess, went into his chambers, and married us.

After that, Dina stayed in Midtown South, but I was sent down to the Ninth, because I speak Spanish and there are a lot of Hispanics there. This is what I found.

The Ninth covers the area from the East River to Broadway and from Fourteenth Street on the north to Houston Street on the south. Living conditions in the area are horrible. Certain areas are poverty-stricken, and the landlords don't keep up the buildings at all. You can go into some of the apartment buildings and they look as if they'd been wrecked in a war.

Pots and pans will be set out all over the place to catch the water that leaks in. Water has been completely shut off in some of the buildings, and you will see people running down to the nearest hydrant, pails in hand, to get water for washing and drinking.

Other buildings in the precinct have been completely abandoned. The landlords have just walked away and left them. They are wrecks, windows are broken out, doors smashed in, stairs falling apart. In just one short block between Avenues B and C, there were fourteen burned-out skeletons of buildings. The awful dirt and smells are hard to imagine unless you've seen and smelled them. There are piles of trash in the halls, rotting garbage, the overpowering odor of urine. Such buildings are used by junkies as "shooting galleries."

Jammed into this slum of slums are people of all races, nationalities, and descriptions. The Bowery, filled with derelicts, is at the southwestern end of the precinct. If you are driving along Houston Street and have to stop for a traffic light, you're almost certain to be approached by a "skell." That's what we call the bums.

The skell will stagger out into the street, waving a disgustingly dirty rag. He'll attempt to rub it over your windshield or side-view mirror, pretending he is cleaning the glass. The skell obviously hasn't washed in weeks, and there's an odor about him that's enough to make you sick. So you give him a dime, a quarter—anything to get rid of him—and he goes and gets himself some more cheap wine.

There is an island in the middle of Houston Street that is maybe four feet wide. You'll find the skells sleeping there at three or four o'clock in the morning, waiting for the crack of dawn to "clean" some more windshields.

Some of these skells are so far gone that they just go out into the street without thinking about the traffic. That's the way some of them get killed. One time, Dina and I were riding a bus going to an Italian festival, and we saw an ambulance and police cars in the street. They were just covering up the remains of a skell who had been crushed to pieces. The sight was so sickening that a woman in the seat behind us in the bus became violently ill.

West of the Bowery and going north along

the streets covered by the Ninth, you find areas in the southern section where Chinese are beginning to settle. Toward the middle of the precinct, along First, Second and Third Avenues, there are a number of ethnic groups: Hungarians, Poles, Jews, and Italians. And then, on the far eastern side, from First Avenue down to the river, there are Hispanics and Blacks.

All of these different people are jammed together like bees in a beehive in this small, run-down section of the city. To make matters worse, a methadone clinic has been set up in the heart of the Polish neighborhood along Second Avenue between Ninth and Tenth Streets. Every Monday, Wednesday, and Friday, the drug addicts gather to get their free methadone, which is supposed to get them off heroin.

They bunch up in a mob about the clinic, blocking the sidewalk so that no one can get past. They mill around, stealing from one another, sometimes killing each other for the methadone. The thing is, if you have a little extra methadone, you can make yourself some money—and some of these addicts will do anything to get it.

Extra cops have to be placed in the area to

try to keep some kind of order on those days. It's a big hassle.

One of the worst parts of this is that the Poles in the neighborhood are stable people. The addicts aren't from their area. They come in from the Bronx, Queens, all over. Once they've gotten their methadone, they won't go home. They hang around from eight in the morning until six at night, trying to see what they can steal from someone else.

They cause enough trouble to make other people stay away. People won't go into the restaurants, with the junkies hanging around. And they don't dare stand on a street corner waiting for a bus. They have to walk some blocks out of their way.

When things are like this, and people live without hope, you are bound to have all kinds of trouble. People living in these conditions become so upset and angry, that they take out their feelings on anyone they see. We cops are out there in uniform, and easy to see, so we sometimes come to stand for everything they hate.

Kids in this area start breaking windows when

they are seven or eight years old, and as they get older they take part in more serious kinds of crime. On night patrol, on the twelve-to-eight shift, it's common to find kids this young out on the streets at three o'clock in the morning.

We stop them and ask them where they live. We ask them what they are doing. And we get the kind of answers you wouldn't believe. They begin by calling us "mother-fucking pigs" and go on from there.

They are like lost puppies with no one to worry about them. No one cares—not even their mothers. If you pick a kid up and take him home and tell the mother you've found him out on the corner at three o'clock, she gets angry and says, "So what?"

What are you going to do to straighten these problems out? Frankly, I don't know. I sometimes think they'll never be straightened out. How on earth can parents, no matter how hard things are, let their kids loose on the city streets at all hours? It must be that the parents don't care. And as long as they don't, these kinds of things are going to happen.

That's a general picture of the Ninth Precinct.

As I said, I never knew that crime could be so bad until I was sent here. In most precincts, you may handle as many as ten or fifteen cases during an eight-hour tour. Here, one night, my partner and I handled thirty calls on one shift.

4

A Wild Tour

That was one tour of duty I'll never forget. I never saw so many things happen in one eight-hour period in my life.

I was on the four-to-twelve that night. That's from four in the afternoon until midnight. I was covering Sector 4, which runs from Seventh to Fourteenth Streets and from Avenue C down to the East River.

Each precinct is divided into sectors. The average sector includes only four or five square blocks. But in the Ninth it was different. There was a large Consolidated Edison plant on one block. Other blocks had been virtually destroyed and abandoned. These were areas where there was little to patrol, and so the northeast sector of the precinct, where I was stationed, was longer than usual.

When we are on patrol, each of us has a code signal so that the Central Communications Division can keep in touch with us. My signal for Sector 4 was "Nine Boy." The numeral always refers to the number of the precinct. The following code word is for the individual cop covering a specific sector.

This tour had hardly started when I got a call from Central. "Nine Boy," Central called. I answered. The dispatcher said there was a man slumped over, perhaps dying from an overdose, on the top floor of a five-story tenement. The building was on Eighth Street between Avenues C and D.

My partner on this tour was Joe McGrath. When we got to the building, we couldn't believe it was possible for anyone to be up there on the top floor. A sign on the front of the building showed that it had been condemned by the Fire Department.

When a building is condemned, the Fire Department uses three different kinds of signs to show how dangerous it is to go into it. The first sign is a plain square. This means that, though the building has been condemned, it is safe to enter. The second sign is a square with a line drawn across it. What this says is: "Beware." You can enter, but there is danger if you do. The third sign is a square with an X in it. This means that the building may be ready to fall down about your ears. Don't go in, no matter what.

The tenement where this man was supposed to be on the top floor was one of those buildings that had the square with warning X in it. We couldn't believe there could be anyone up there, and we called the Center back to double check. "Are you sure this is the right building?" I asked.

Yes, he said, he was sure. The Department had had two or three calls about someone who was trapped up on the fifth floor, making noises there. So Joe McGrath and I had to go in.

We started up the stairway, and I've never seen a more rotten set of stairs. There were gaps where one or two steps had rotted away and fallen down into the stairwell. We had to leap over those gaps. And we never knew if the step we were going to land on would hold us.

Joe would jump over a gap, and find the next step solid enough to hold him. Then he would lean back down and stretch out his nightstick. I would grab the end of the nightstick, and he would pull as I would jump. As I did, he would go up to the next step, because we never wanted to both be on one step at the same time. We knew that, if a step should break under us, we could fall two or three stories. And that would be the end of us.

It took us some time to make the climb, stepping as lightly as we could and jumping across the gaps in the rotten staircase. Finally, we got to the top of the building and found a young junkie slumped over there. He had been stabbed in the back.

I don't know how he ever got up there, what he was doing there, or what happened to him. Probably, he went up to give himself a fix. He must have had a friend with him—a friend who knifed him to steal the drug he had.

The junkie was in pretty bad shape, and we put through a call for an ambulance. Then we had the job of getting the ambulance men up those broken stairs and carrying the stabbed junkie down.

The ambulance driver and his attendant put the man in a chair, and we walked him down as far as we could. Then we came to the first gap in the stairs. The ambulance men opened the chair out into a stretcher and slid it down over the gap until one of us on a solid step below could grab it. That's the way we got the junkie out. We had to leap over the gaps in the stairs and pass the stretcher along from hand to hand. Then the ambulance crew rushed the man off to a hospital, and he lived. All the bad guys live.

Of course, the stabbing was never solved. When the junkie finally came to in the hospital, he didn't know where he was, what had happened to him, or who had done it. He must have been so spaced out he couldn't remember anything.

In the meantime, there was an hour of paperwork for us. We had to fill out an aided card, giving the details of what we had done. Then we had to call the Missing Persons Bureau, because there was no identification on him. There was no way of telling who he was and he might be someone Missing Persons had been asked to look for.

We had hardly finished this and gotten back on the street when Central Communications was dinging "Nine Boy" again. This time, it was a Code 10–31. All "30" codes—that is, anything like a ten with a number in the thirties behind it —means that there is a crime of some kind being committed at that very moment.

This time, an apartment in a three-story building on Eighth Street was being robbed. According to the report, the burglar was trying to get away by coming down the fire escape. We rushed to the building. Two cops in a radio car came up on the other side, trying to box the burglar in so he could not escape. But he must have seen us coming, because, when we got there, he had gone back up to the roof. We just got a quick look at this figure on the roof, and we went up as fast as we could.

We had our walkie-talkies, and we kept in touch with the radio-car patrolmen coming up the other side. But when we got to the rooftop, the burglar was gone. All we got was that one look at his shadowy figure. Those guys can run like rabbits, and they jump from rooftop to rooftop with amazing speed. This one had had a head start on us and had vanished over the roof-tops before we could get there.

Since he had broken in the apartment door to gain entrance, we had to guard the place until the owner arrived. When the owner showed up, we told him what had happened. Then we told him to get in touch with an officer at the pre-cinct, who could tell him what kind of locks to get to make his apartment safer. And, of course, we had to fill out another report.

Back on the street again, it was one thing after another. The action never stopped. We had a heart-attack case and called another am-bulance. There were accidents on the highway, and we had to give out summonses. There were robberies in the neighborhood, and we had to serve as backup to other policemen. (Anytime there is a crime of violence in progress, we back one another up. You don't walk into a dangerous situation alone if you can help it.)

It went on like that, it seemed, forever. We were constantly on the run. Joe McGrath and I wound up handling some thirty cases before our shift was up, at midnight. Thirty cases in one eight-hour shift. It was unbelievable.

5

Some Strange
Cases

In a district like the Ninth, there are a lot of
psychotic persons, and we were always getting
strange calls. I would say that perhaps 20 per
cent of the calls that we received were un-
founded. Some of them seemed at times like de-
liberate setups. And if you fall for the trap, you
can lose your life if you are not careful.

I remember one night when I was on radio-
car patrol with Joe McGrath. He was usually my
partner. We got a call that a sniper had been
spotted on the roof of a building on Fourth
Street between Avenues C and D.

We drove to the tenement next door to the one where the sniper was supposed to be. Tenants in the building, some of whom had phoned in the alarm, were highly excited. Yes, they told us, there's a sniper on that roof right next door; some of us have seen him.

This was another of those five-story tenement buildings, and Joe McGrath and I hurried up to the roof. We ran across the roof to the edge adjoining the building where the sniper was supposed to be.

It was a black night, and we couldn't see a thing. Normally, I suppose, we might have jumped before we looked, not wanting to give ourselves away to the sniper. But, fortunately for us, we had our flashlights with us. We turned them on to see what the roof was like where the sniper had been reported.

There was no roof there.

Our flashlights showed just the wooden two-by-four rafters that had supported the roof; but the whole roof had collapsed. If we had jumped in the dark, we would have ended up dead five stories down in the basement. It was enough to send some cold chills up your spine.

Obviously, there never could have been a

sniper on the roof that wasn't there. How had the alarm started? Who had started it? Was someone trying to bring us to our deaths? We never could find out. Once a story like that gets started, people become frightened and alarmed. They *think* they saw what they were supposed to see. If they didn't see it themselves, they knew somebody else who said he had seen the sniper. Trying to trace how something like this gets started is a hopeless task. The more you question people who had been so *sure* about what they saw, the less they remember, until the whole thing just vanishes into thin air.

Another time, I came off duty at midnight, and it was about 1 A.M. when I got home. Our apartment is in Waterside Plaza, overlooking the East River at Twenty-fifth Street. Dina had come off duty earlier and was already there. She was looking out our window, from which there is a clear view of the East Side marine basin.

"There's a fishing boat down there," she said. "Is anybody supposed to be working on that boat tonight?"

"I don't think so," I said.

I went to the window and looked out. There was a man on the boat, acting strangely. He was running back and forth the length of the boat, grabbing things and throwing them over the side.

"That doesn't look right," I said. "I'd better call the dispatcher."

I put the call through, but the dispatcher was cautious. She wanted to make certain I was a cop and asked for my registry number. I gave it to her.

"Okay," she said, "I believe you. I'll send a radio car."

I went back to the window, where Dina was standing. The fellow on the boat was still working like a demon, pitching everything he could get his hands on over the side.

"By the time the dispatcher gets a radio car here, that guy could have the engine overboard," Dina said. "We'd better go down and stop him ourselves."

We left the apartment and ran across to the basin. By the time we got there, some attendants at the Gulf service station had noticed what was happening and had gotten the guy off the boat. But they were having a terrific struggle with him. When some of these kooks lose their minds, they have extraordinary strength. This fellow the Gulf men had taken off the boat was more than they could handle. Dina waded right into the middle of the struggle. And she had everything under control by the time the radio-car cops arrived.

It turned out the man hadn't been trying to loot the boat. He had just lost his senses, and in a mindless way, had been having himself some fun.

The next morning, when we got up, we saw the crew of the fishing boat out on a raft. They were trying to recover the things that had been thrown overboard. There must have been at least one hundred life jackets floating on the water. The whole basin around the boat was orange-colored with them.

Another night, I was on radio-car patrol with Sergeant Stephen Friedland. We got a call, Code 10–31, reporting a burglary in progress at the public school on Ninth Street between Avenues B and C. We were on Eighth Street and Avenue C when we got the call.

"Turn down Ninth and let's go," the Sergeant said.

I made a left turn into Ninth. When we reached the school, the custodian came out, waving his arms.

"He just went in through that window," he yelled to us, pointing to a ground-floor window where the screen had been ripped out.

Sergeant Friedland and I both drew our guns. We ran up to the open window and stationed ourselves on either side of it. Looking in, we could just see a dim figure. He looked huge, a good six feet tall. He was coming toward the window as if he was going to try to get out.

"We're police! Freeze!" we shouted.

Instead of freezing, he took off, running back through the building. We jumped through the window after him. He dashed up the front stairwell, with both of us chasing him. He ran down one hall, up another set of stairs, then down again. It was a chase through the whole school like the final, wild scramble you see in a detective story on television.

Finally, we cornered him in the basement. He tried to hide behind a pile of garbage cans, but we spotted him and called to him to come out. When he rose up, he turned and faced us, waving a crowbar in his hands.

"Drop that crowbar or I'll shoot," I ordered.

He waved it as if he was going to throw it at me. But when I pointed my gun right at him, he decided to give up. He dropped the crowbar, which made a loud clank as it hit the concrete floor. Then I arrested him for the burglary of a public school.

As it turned out, he was an escapee from the Bellevue Hospital Psychiatric Ward. He was a Spanish kid, only fifteen years old, and already over six feet tall. We were surprised. He had looked older and bigger and more menacing when we had first seen him in the gloom of the basement.

After I had finished all the paperwork, I took him back to the Bellevue ward where he belonged. They put him in a correctional section, behind bars. A policeman was put on guard over him, and I went home about 1 A.M.

In the morning, I had to get up at six-thirty to relieve the policeman who was guarding my school burglar. I had to take the kid to court, but he wouldn't come out. They had already tested him at Bellevue and decided that he wasn't insane at all. But the kid was arguing that he was and that he belonged in Bellevue.

He didn't want to be taken to court and have to face his punishment.

As a result, I had to go in and drag him out. This isn't as simple as it may sound. You can't go into Bellevue with a loaded gun, because you can't tell what some of the patients there may do. While you're trying to get the cuffs on your prisoner, they could very well snatch your gun and begin firing. So I had to take all the bullets out of my gun and put the empty gun back in my holster before I went in. Then, if someone grabbed it, at least there couldn't be any shooting.

After I had done that, I went in to get my prisoner. He tried to make trouble, but I got the cuffs on him. Then he came along quietly enough.

He was a wise guy. I knew that since he had tried to pass himself off as a mental case to escape being punished. But I didn't realize just how much of a wise guy he was until we were on the way out of the ward. Then he leaned close to me and whispered, "Officer, don't forget."

"Forget what?" I asked.

He put his lips up to my ear and whispered, "Don't forget to put the bullets back in the gun."

When we got to Juvenile Court, on Twenty-second Street near Lexington Avenue, it seemed that everybody in the place knew this kid. The woman entering his name on the record recognized him. The attendant in the courtroom knew him. Even some of the other prisoners who were being held for hearings recognized him. "Hey, how are you?" they'd ask him. He had been in trouble so often, it was like old home week.

Court attendants kept him under lock and key while I went back to the school to get the custodian. He had to sign a formal complaint and identify my prisoner as the burglar.

When the hearing was held, the custodian told the judge, "Yeah, he's the one who broke the screen off the window, opened the window, and went in."

A Legal Aid Society lawyer represented the youth. They went through some plea bargaining, knocking the charge down from burglary to breaking and entering. The boy, of course, was willing to make all kinds of promises. "Yes, sir, judge, I'll go straight this time. Yes, sir, judge, I've learned my lesson, and I'll never do anything like that again." That kind of stuff.

The judge, however, had heard all this before. This was about the third time he'd had this same kid before him. He was annoyed at his song and dance. So, he sent the kid to a correctional facility upstate, where he was put to work on the farms until he was sixteen. That was about all that could be done with him, since he was a juvenile.

Sergeant Friedland and I both got citations for Excellent Police Duty for the way we had handled the case. That always helps on your record.

6

The Extra Sense

Some police officers have an extra sense, an instinct, that tells them when something is wrong. Dina has it. She and I will be walking down the street and she'll say, "Look at that guy; he's up to something." I will look at him and not be able to see any sign that he's different from anyone else on the street. But, nine times out of ten, Dina will be right.

Patrolman Paul Pawelko, with whom I have shared many tours of duty, has the same kind of sense that Dina has. It seemed that every time I went on patrol with Pawelko I ended up making an arrest.

I remember the first time we were on patrol together in a radio car. We had the four-to-midnight shift. We were driving along slowly, and suddenly Pawelko said, "Say, Acha, see that guy over there? He doesn't look right."

We stopped the car and got out. The man didn't move.

"Hey, Buddy, what are you doing here?" I asked him.

He didn't say a thing, just stood there; and Pawelko frisked him. He came out with a knife blade almost as long as a bayonet. I exclaimed, "Oh, my God!" I was so surprised I couldn't help it.

Another time—this was April 7, 1976, after I had been transferred from the Ninth to the Midtown North precinct—Pawelko and I were cruising south along Second Avenue near Fortieth Street about nine o'clock at night. We had Sector Charlie David, which covers from 38th to 46th Streets and from Lexington Avenue to the FDR Drive. We were going slowly to get a look at the shop windows on both sides of the street. We wanted to make certain that everything was safe and no stores were being looted.

Another police car passed us. Pawelko said, "He just turned his lights on. Let's follow him."

I made a quick turn at Thirty-eighth Street, and we spotted the rotating lights up the street. We headed for the scene and pulled up in front of a building where the doorman was waving, pointing behind us. We looked and saw a tall teen-ager running in the direction from which we had just come.

We all piled out of the cars. There were the two policemen in the car that had passed us, and Pawelko and myself. We gave chase on foot. This kid was a pretty fast runner, but I was faster and finally ran him down. Then he gave us a terrific struggle. It took all four of us to get him down and get the handcuffs on him.

We took this big, strong kid to the station house and locked him up. Then we found out what had happened. It seems that a big honcho of American Airlines had been going to get his car. The youth and a girl who was with him went up to him and asked for enough money "to get home." When the man refused and started down the ramp to get his car, they jumped him, banged him up against the iron railing of the ramp, and beat him up. They took his wallet with fifty dollars in it and all his credit cards.

As with so many cases, the real trouble for me started after the arrest. The next morning, the older brother of the teen-ager I had arrested showed up. It seems that the kid had had his older brother's ID card on him, showing he was twenty-one.

"Hey," the brother argued with me, "you've got to let him go. He is not him. That's me. And I'm not arrested."

I tell you, they will try anything. I wasn't having any part of this.

"Listen, pal," I told the older brother, "all I know is that I got his fingerprints and whether they match the name or not, makes no difference to me. Whatever way it turns out, I've got *him* for what he did."

It turned into a regular courtroom mess that took up about four days of my time. The Legal Aid Society lawyer wouldn't handle the case. I don't know why. Then the boy's mother, who lived out in the Midwest somewhere, called up one of the big law firms and another lawyer showed up. The mother must have told the lawyer that her son was a good boy and would never do anything bad, but as soon as the lawyer found out what really had happened, he, too, just waved good-by. Finally, the mother came up with a third lawyer, who agreed to act.

In the meantime, I had to go before the grand jury and testify. The airlines big shot testified too, describing what had happened. The theft of the credit cards alone made it a grand-larceny case, because a thief can get a lot of money out of using credit cards. In the end, the kid was indicted by the grand jury; there was the usual plea bargaining; and he got sent up for a three-to-five-year term. That meant that, with good behavior, he could be out and on the street again in little more than a year.

You never know, when you are on patrol, what can happen in the next minute. It can be the quietest night, the patrol can be dull and routine, with nothing happening. Then, in the next second, all hell can break loose.

It was like that one night when Pawelko and I were ending our tour in the Ninth. We were on the four-to-midnight shift. Nothing seemed to be happening, and Pawelko said, "It's eleven-thirty and time we headed for home."

We turned back toward the East Fifth Street station house, and suddenly we saw a man staggering toward a cop standing on a corner. As we pulled up, we heard the man say, "I've just been robbed and stabbed."

"Come on, get in the car, and we'll take you to the station house and call an ambulance," I said.

When we got the victim to the station house, a few minutes later, we opened his shirt. He had been stabbed all right. The wound was right in the center of his chest, ugly and deep, the blood pumping right out.

We got some paper towels, wadded them, and pressed them into the slash in the man's chest to stop the bleeding as much as possible.

"Come on," Pawelko said, "we better not wait for an ambulance. The way this guy looks, we better get him to a hospital right away."

We bundled the man back into the police car and raced to the Emergency Ward at Bellevue Hospital. We were just in time, the doctors told us later. They said that we had saved the man's life by getting him there so quickly.

That is one of the great satisfactions I get out of being a policeman. When you can help somebody, especially when you can actually *save a life*, you get a good, rewarding feeling. The job then becomes worth all the hassles.

And there are always hassles, even in a case like this. When we came back to the station house from Bellevue, I filled out all the papers on the case simply because nobody else wanted to. This kept me late, and so I put in for fifteen minutes overtime. Then the crazy desk sergeant that we had screamed at me. Why did I put in for fifteen minutes overtime?

"Is it coming out of your pocket?" I asked him.

"Yes," he said.

That really upset me. I had felt good about the case because we had saved the man's life. Now this desk martinet was making something cheap out of it. You get people like that sometimes.

"Look," I said, "just tear the damn thing up. I'm going home."

49

There was another night almost like this one, when nothing much seemed to be happening—and then, all of a sudden, we found ourselves in a city version of a Wild West chase.

This night, I was on radio-car patrol with Officer Edward Jeorgenson. We were working Sector 4 ("Nine Boy") in the Ninth Precinct again. We had patrolled our area, then hit the FDR Drive headed south. We turned off on Sixth Street to go back to our sector. As we did, a Buick Riviera came toward us from the opposite direction with no lights on.

I turned on our flashing lights and yelled to him, "Hey, buddy, you know you can see better if you turn your lights on."

"Okay, officer," he replied, very politely, and switched on his lights.

We turned off the flashing lights on the top of our car, and we hadn't gone more than about ten feet when a man came running out into the street.

"Stop him, officer!" he yelled. "He just robbed me!"

"Hurry!" I said. "Get in the car."

The man climbed into the back of the patrol car, and Jeorgenson grabbed the phone and called Central Communications. He reported the make of the car, and what had happened, and told them we were taking up the chase.

We whirled around to follow the Buick Riviera, which was now speeding south down the FDR Drive. He had such a head start on us that we lost him on the drive. In the meantime, the First Precinct, where Dina was working, had picked up our call. They were on the air to us.

"Is it a gray Buick Riviera?" they asked.

"Yes," we told them.

"Does the driver have a beard, long hair, and a mustache?"

"Yes," we said again.

So the dispatcher at the First Precinct notified Central Communications: "We are now pursuing the Buick towards the Brooklyn Battery Tunnel. Have the Brooklyn police set up a roadblock on the other side."

We raced into the tunnel, and by the time we got through it, they had the Buick Riviera stopped.

I dashed over.

"This is my collar," I shouted, meaning my arrest.

"Oh, no," said the sergeant from the First,

"you lost the chase and we picked it up. It's our collar."

They were right, of course. Once you lose sight of the person you are chasing and someone else picks him up, the arrest belongs to the other person. So we all went back to the First Precinct, where we booked the prisoner. I got another citation for Excellent Police Duty out of it, and some of the others got citations as well.

7

Handling a Riot

Anytime some seventy-five thousand people, living in the worst conditions, are packed together in an area of only eight tenths of a square mile, there is danger. All you have to do is look around you at the run-down tenements and the rows of wrecked and abandoned buildings. Those buildings, with all the windows broken out, stare at you with vacant eyes. It is almost as if they could speak, describing the poverty and desperation of the neighborhood.

It is no wonder that, in conditions like this, you have violence. The terrible poverty of the area makes this certain. Every month when the welfare checks come out, there are muggings, robberies, thefts. The poor rip off the poor. People have to live any way they can.

This is the pattern of life in the Ninth. There are so many out of work, scratching for a living any way they can get it. People fight hard for the few jobs there are. This is what led to a riot in June 1975. In trying to put it down, I was injured for the first time since I joined the force.

I wasn't supposed to be on duty that night. I was filling in for an officer who had reported sick. My partner and I were covering Sector H, Henry, when the call came over the radio, Code 10–13. That means a police officer is in trouble and needs help. The location given was Seventeenth Street and Park Avenue South.

That wasn't in our precinct, but it was close. The borderline between the Ninth and the Thirteenth precincts is Fourteenth Street. We were cruising in our radio car close to the border when we got the call. So we turned on the flashing lights and the siren and hurried over.

When we arrived at the scene, there was a real battle going on. A mob that must have numbered nearly one hundred young men—and some women, too—had gathered in front of a union headquarters. They had gathered there waiting for union officials to come out of a meeting they were holding inside their headquarters, but tempers had gotten out of hand.

The trouble stemmed from the fact that the union was virtually closed to outsiders. Membership in many unions is handed down from father to son, or to close relatives of members. Those who don't have this special "in" can't get a union card. And without that union card, they can't get work.

The mob we met was made up mostly of young white men in tattered jeans, with heavy beards on their faces. They looked like leftovers from the Vietnam War protests, and they were shouting obscenities and waving fists, sticks, and clubs.

The Thirteenth Precinct had sent four cops over to try to keep order. I don't know whether it was the sight of the uniforms that angered the mob. They probably got the idea that the cops were stationed there to side with the union officials, which wasn't the case at all. They were just trying to keep order and see that no one got hurt.

Anyway, by the time we arrived, the demonstrators were cursing the "mother-fucking pigs," and they had started to attack the policemen and beat them up. They had knocked down a sergeant, and there were about ten of them piled on top of him, beating him with their fists.

We stopped the radio car, and my 'partner and I jumped into the fight. I made for the bunch of rioters that were piled on top of the sergeant. I had my nightstick out, and I began to hit at the butts and legs of the sergeant's attackers. A nightstick is a great leveler. When it hit them, they yelped and started to rise up. Then I yanked some of them off the heap.

The pile that had been on top of the sergeant had begun to unravel when I felt this horrible pain across the middle of my back. I whirled around and saw this bearded guy waving a heavy cane. He had swung it back, ready to hit me again, when I tackled him and pulled the cane out of his hands.

As I did, I felt another horrible pain across the back of my knees. It was as if the world had fallen in on me, and I started to crumble. Another of the rioters, when my back was turned, had slammed me across the back of my knees with a piece of two-by-four timber that he was waving like a club. The blow was a heavy one. The pain was excruciating.

All I could think of was that I had to keep my feet no matter what happened. If I fell, I could be trampled to death by the boots of this unruly mob. Staggering, I managed to stay upright. I laid about me with my nightstick, warding off some blows, taking some, and delivering some counterblows of my own. The women in this crowd were as bad as the men. They had two-by-fours in their hands, and they were clubbing away viciously.

Some of us might have been killed, or at least much more badly injured, if police cars hadn't come screaming to the scene from both precincts. About thirty policemen piled out of the cars and into the mob, wielding their nightsticks. This new attack routed the rioters.

Most of them threw away their clubs and took to their heels. Three of the ringleaders were arrested. Two of the union officials whom the mob had gotten to had been beaten so badly they had to be taken to a hospital. Another policeman and myself were taken there too.

The other policeman had had his head split

open from a blow he had taken. I had big black-and-blue marks all across my chest, back, and the backs of my knees from the beating I had taken during the fight.

The way one of the rioters was arrested was strange. We were in the emergency ward, getting examined and patched up. Some of the policemen who had brought us there were questioning one of the injured union officials. They were trying to get a description from him of the man who had beaten him up.

In the middle of the questioning, a tall, bearded brute came limping in from the street. He could hardly walk, because he was one on whom our nightsticks had really done a job. The union official looked up and recognized him at once.

"That's the SOB who beat me up!" he cried out. "That's him!"

So the guy not only got treated for his injuries; he got arrested, too.

8

Two Officers Killed

In wretched neighborhoods like the Ninth, tensions are increased by language differences that help to block out understanding between police and the people who live there. Often, a strange kind of love-hate relationship develops between them.

On the one hand, the people want the police to protect them. On the other, the conditions of their lives make them angry and untrusting. When you add to that the fact that many policemen can't speak their language, it is easy to see how misunderstandings sometimes develop. The uniform we wear makes us seem to them like symbols of a system that treats them badly. So some of these people will take things out on us.

I answered a routine call one day and came out of a tenement to find my patrol car all bashed up.

I was on an eight-to-four shift with Joe McGrath that day. We got a call to go to a tenement on Fifth Street between Avenues C and D, where some children had been reported abandoned. Joe and I investigated, and this is what we found:

A woman in the building, the mother of two children, had gone into a hospital to have another baby. She had left her children with her next-door neighbor, with whom she was friendly. The neighbor had agreed to take care of the kids until the mother returned from the hospital. That was all there was to it. There should have been no problem.

But it seems that a couple of other women, who claimed to be the friends of the mother, wanted to take the children. They had complained to the precinct that the children had no one to care for them. They had tried to get the

children from the neighbor, and she had refused
to give them up.

As soon as Joe and I found out what the situation was, I went downstairs to another apartment, where there was a telephone, and called
the mother in the hospital. Yes, she said, she had
left her children with her neighbor. That's where
she wanted them to stay.

I had hardly gotten this straight when I heard
Joe McGrath yelling: "Carlos, come down quick.
They're wrecking the police car."

I ran down the stairs and found a crowd gathered around the car. Someone had taken some
bricks and thrown them right through the rear
window, smashing out all the glass. They had
really done a job on it.

Since this was a Hispanic neighborhood and I
speak Spanish, I asked the people in the crowd
what had happened, why anyone would want to
batter the police car. They began to talk all at
once as soon as they found I understood them.
Out of the babble, I finally gathered that the
whole neighborhood had been aroused when Joe
and I arrived in the police car, because they
thought we were going to take the children

away. I explained to them that we weren't going to take the children away. The children belonged right where they were and that was where they were going to stay.

That calmed them down, but when I tried to find out who had smashed the window of the police car, I got nowhere. Nobody knew anything. Joe and I always suspected that the damage was done by a couple of Spanish teen-agers, twins who were always giving us trouble. They had been on the street when we went into the tenement, and they weren't there when we came back. However, all we had was a suspicion. We could never prove anything.

This incident has always stuck in my mind. It is a perfect example of how difficult it is for people in such neighborhoods to understand the police. They want protection. They want the police to shield them against robbers, muggers, burglars. Yet when police show up suddenly to settle some minor hassle like this, they become instantly fearful about what the police are going to do. They become easily upset—even to the point of violence.

We tried our best in the Ninth Precinct to reach a better understanding with the residents of the neighborhood. A special Neighborhood Police Team was formed under one of our best officers, Sergeant Frederick Reddy, fifty-one, a twenty-eight-year veteran of the force. The team was an all-volunteer group. Reddy and his partner, Patrolman Andrew Glover, thirty-four, who had been on the force six years, went out into the community to try to establish a better understanding with the people.

They and other members of their team went out on radio-car and foot patrols. They met with youth groups. Reddy himself, in plain clothes, would often walk the area on foot, going from door to door, talking to the people and asking them about their problems.

"Reddy and Glover helped us a lot," some of the people said. You heard that over and over again. Reddy and Glover were two of the most admired, best liked men in the Ninth.

I knew both of these officers well. Glover was a wonderful person, understanding and considerate. I will never forget the accidental run-in I had with him when I was a rookie cop. I spotted a gypsy taxicab parked too close to a corner, where it was partially blocking a crosswalk, and I ticketed it.

Shortly afterward, Glover approached me with the ticket in his hand.

"Is this yours?" he asked.

"Yes, that's mine," I told him.

"Do you know this cab belongs to the Anti-Crime Unit?" Glover asked.

I was totally surprised. No one had told me that the Anti-Crime Unit was using gypsy cabs in their undercover work.

"I didn't know anything about it," I told Glover, "and there was nothing in the window to make me think the cab might belong to the anti-crime force. Here, give the ticket back to me and I'll make out a '49' on it."

That's the form you have to fill out and file, telling your boss that you goofed, you made a mistake. Glover was very nice about it, and he vouched for me, telling my superiors I had just been doing my job and there was no way I could have known. I was just a rookie then, and I always felt grateful to him for the way he acted.

I recall all of this because of what happened on September 16, 1975. I was working an eight-to-four that day, and I was late getting back to the East Fifth Street station house before going home. As I entered, I met Sergeant Reddy. He was just about to leave, and he was in uniform.

He was always in plain clothes when he went around the neighborhood, and I was surprised to see him in uniform. So I said to him, "Sergeant, what's up? Where are you going today?"

"Oh," he said, "I just thought I'd take a regular patrol today to roam around and see what's happening."

"Gee," I said, "I haven't seen you in uniform since I've been here."

He drew himself up a little proudly, making a game of it. "How do I look?" he asked.

"You look fine," I told him. "You look just great."

That night, I was home looking at television when a news flash came on about ten o'clock. It reported that two police officers had been killed on the Lower East Side.

That didn't register with me as hard as it might have at first. There are other precincts besides the Ninth on the Lower East Side. But then the 11 o'clock news came on, and the announcer identified the slain policemen as Sergeant Reddy and Patrolman Glover.

It was like a kick in the stomach. I sat there

in a state of shock. At first, I couldn't believe it. Here I had seen Reddy only a few hours before, drawing himself up erect and proud in his uniform and asking me how he looked.

I found out later that Reddy and Glover had been driving along East Fifth Street between Avenues A and B when they spotted this banged-up parked car in front of 537 East Fifth. The car looked as if it might have been damaged in an accident. There were some men inside it.

Reddy and Glover pulled the radio car to a stop just in front of the parked vehicle, and Glover walked back to see what was the matter. As he did, the men in the car came out, firing.

Glover never had a chance. They found him later, slumped over the trunk of the car. A bullet had been fired into the back of his head at point-blank range.

When the firing started, Sergeant Reddy scrambled out of the radio car. He managed to get off a few shots. Then a bullet struck him in the chest, and he fell down dead on the pavement.

9

Grim Days

The Ninth Precinct station house was like a morgue the day after Reddy and Glover were killed. Whenever a fellow officer is slain, it hits you hard. In this case, the whole force in the Ninth felt the blow even more than usual, because Reddy and Glover were two of the best-liked officers in the whole precinct.

You found it hard to believe that the lives of two such admirable men could have been snuffed out like *that*—as quickly as you can snap your fingers.

It was a tribute to the job Reddy and Glover

had done that many residents of the area felt the same sense of loss and outrage that we did. Some of them would come up to us on the street to express their sympathy. Others even came into the station house and told us, "We hope you get the bastards that did this."

One of those most affected was Anna Hmelo, a Czech woman. She had come to the United States in 1929. She had raised her children on the Lower East Side, and she was the superintendent of an apartment house on the block where Reddy and Glover were killed.

She recalled afterward how Reddy had used to stop and talk with her while he was making his rounds.

"Hello, Mama, how are you today?" he'd say.

"Okay," she would tell him.

"That's good," he'd reply.

It got to be like a little game between them. After these preliminaries, Reddy would stand and talk to her for several minutes before he drifted on along the block to hold similar conversations with others.

As muggings and violence increased in the neighborhood, Anna made it a rule not to go out of her apartment after six o'clock at night. And so she was in her home, sitting snug and secure by her window, the night Reddy and Glover were murdered.

She heard the shots and looked out just in time to see Reddy fall. Forgetting caution, she abandoned her rule about not going out into dark streets and ran from her apartment. She knelt down by Reddy and whispered, "Sergeant Reddy, I know you."

Reddy didn't stir. He was already dead.

As the truth dawned on Anna, she turned and fled back into her apartment. Though it was September and the weather was mild, she started to shiver from shock. Her teeth chattered as if she had taken a chill in the heart of winter. She bundled herself up in sweaters and shawls—and still couldn't get warm.

She was so horrified—and so terrified—that she remained locked up in her apartment for two days.

That gives some idea of the effect this outrageous deed had on many of the residents of the Ninth Precinct.

In the station house itself, the mood was grim. Usually, there is a certain amount of horseplay, with cops ribbing one another and having a bit of good-natured fun. But not on this day. Nobody felt like talking. There was a grim, determined look on every face.

We were all set on getting the killers, no matter how much effort it took. Every one of us, when we came off our regular tours of duty, put on civilian clothes and spent extra hours roaming the streets. We talked to various contacts, listened to the gossip in seedy bars. We were determined that somewhere, somehow, we were going to pick up a clue that would lead us to the slayers.

I had been scheduled to leave for my annual two-weeks' training with the Marine Corps Reserve. But there was no way I was going to take off at this time. I notified my marine commander, and I got into quite a hassle about it. With the Marines, the Marines comes first, no matter what. No excuses are accepted. But this was one time it wasn't going to come first. I had quite a job making them understand that.

Since I speak Spanish and we wanted to get as much information as we could from the Hispanic community, I volunteered to help man the phones as an interpreter at the 20th Precinct. That's the Manhattan Robbery Squad, and that was where special phone numbers were set up for persons to call us if they wished to volunteer information.

I manned the phones for three or four days, and I took a number of calls from Spanish-speaking informants. One of them, I think, may have been important.

A Hispanic woman who lived in the Ninth called and asked me, "Do you remember the robbery last week in that liquor store on Avenue B?"

"Sure, I remember," I told her.

Her voice sank to a whisper. "Well," she said, "you remember there were three gunmen, one Hispanic and two Blacks? I think they're the same ones that shot Reddy and Glover."

It sounded as if it might be a good tip, and I passed it along to the detectives handling the case. I don't know whether it actually helped them, but my woman informant may have been at least partially right. (It turned out later that the actual killer of Reddy and Glover was the Hispanic leader of a holdup gang that had pulled off a number of jobs in the Ninth.)

Before the case was solved, however, I ended up in the hospital again. I was injured in a crazy accident that happened while I was on the way to Sergeant Reddy's funeral.

Whenever a police officer is killed in line of duty, the Department turns out in force to show its respect. In this case, the shootings occurred on a Tuesday or a Wednesday. The funerals had to be scheduled for different days because members of the Department couldn't be in two places at once. I went to Glover's funeral on Saturday, and on Monday we were all going to Sergeant Reddy's funeral, out on Long Island.

The Patrolmen's Benevolent Association had rented half a dozen buses to carry the several hundred policemen who were going to the funeral. These were high-level buses with a glass panel in front. They looked almost like double-deckers.

We started out along the Southern State Parkway with a big convoy of police cars in front and the buses in line behind them. I don't know what was the matter with the bus driver we had. There must have been something wrong with him. He would slow down, then he would speed up. There was no reason for it. All he had to do was to drive along nice and stay in line.

But suddenly he began to drive fast, as if he

were going to the races or something. He began to pass some of the other buses. He kept weaving in and out until he had passed about four of the buses in the line.

Now, the overpasses along the parkway are arched—high in the middle, lower at the ends. Because of this and the height of the buses, our drivers had been told to keep to the middle lane. This kook who was driving our bus didn't pay any attention to that. Finally, he pulled out to pass again, couldn't get back into the roomier, middle lane in time—and there was a terrific crash.

The bottom of the overpass sheered off the whole top of the bus.

I was sitting right behind this crazy driver, and when the top of the bus was sliced off, I was showered with glass from the front panel. I had cuts on my face and hands, and I think I swallowed a couple of tiny particles that flew into my mouth. I was just lucky none of the glass went into my eyes, for I was just covered with a shower of splinters.

Even so, I was more fortunate than some others. The policeman who was sitting right behind me had the seat under the front end of the luggage rack. The pipes that form the rack were torn loose and came crashing down on his head. They tore his scalp right open.

Another policeman was even more unlucky. He was sitting in the rear of the bus, right under the air conditioner. When the top was torn off, the air conditioner fell right down on top of him. It almost crushed him to death.

Six of us were hurt so badly that we had to be hospitalized. The rest were just shaken up a little. But, of course, none of us made it to Sergeant Reddy's funeral.

It was some five or six weeks afterward that the Department broke the case. Either from my tip or other information, detectives focused pretty quickly on a gang leader named José Velez. He and two or three gunmen associated with him, Blacks and Hispanics, had pulled off a number of holdups in the area. Since Velez had a previous record, we were all supplied with his picture, taken from police files. We carried that mug shot everywhere we went, trying to locate Velez.

The break finally came from an arrest another policeman in the Ninth had made about a week before the shootings. He had nabbed a suspect who was carrying a gun. Investigation indicated he had been a member of the Velez team in some of their holdups.

In trouble himself, the prisoner wanted to make a deal. So he admitted he knew the two gunmen involved in the Reddy-Glover murders. They were, he said, Velez and a companion, Frank Seguera. Velez and Seguera were holed up in a brownstone on Nineteenth Street. They were heavily armed, the informant said, and it wouldn't be easy to take them.

Naturally, once we had this information, all of the uniformed cops in the Ninth were eager to get in on the action. But the Department handled the case very carefully. Our superiors realized we were too wound up, too eager to avenge Reddy and Glover. And so they wouldn't let any of us in on the final act.

Everything was handled by the detectives of the homicide squad. They covered the brownstone in force. Then, since they didn't want to have to storm the place and risk a shoot-out, they worked out a way to get Velez and Seguera from building on their own.

They arranged for a tip to be telephoned by a supposed friend.

"The cops know where you are, and they're

coming to get you," this "friend" said. "You better get out quick."

Velez and Seguera fell for it. They came running out of the building. The detectives had them surrounded, dead in their gun sights.

Even so, one of them hurled an old-fashioned, German-made hand grenade at one of the detectives. Fortunately, it fell into the gutter and didn't go off. That ended the pair's attempt at resistance. The detectives clamped handcuffs on them and dragged them away.

Velez was convicted of second-degree murder and sentenced to twenty-five years to life in prison. Seguera got off more lightly, since it had been determined Velez did all the shooting. Seguera wasn't tried for the murders, but he was tried and convicted for participating in a robbery with Velez. For this, he, too, drew a long term in prison.

10

Corruption

When I entered the Police Department, in 1973, it had been badly shaken up by a probe of corruption. A state investigating committee known as the Knapp Commission had discovered widespread payoffs. Bookies and numbers runners in some precincts were regularly shaken down for "protection" money. This guaranteed they would not be arrested. The monthly booty so collected was known as "the pad." It was divided among the cops who took part in the dealings according to their rank. In some of the worst instances, large amounts of heroin taken in drug arrests were squirreled out by corrupt cops—and then sold on the street. That was the absolute depth of corruption. There could hardly be anything worse than a policeman becoming a narcotics peddler.

The Knapp Commission concluded that corruption in the Department was just not a case of "a few rotten apples in the barrel," the usual alibi. Instead, it argued, a large part of the barrel had become rotten.

So, by the time I entered the Department, a special emphasis had been placed on honesty. A strong drive was under way to root out corrupt policemen. Everybody was jittery. And anyone with any sense, it seemed to me, would take special care to keep his or her nose clean.

I certainly saw no signs of corruption while I worked in the Ninth. There was no such thing as "the pad." Everywhere I went, I paid. So did fellows like Joe McGrath and Paul Pawelko. None of us would take anything.

Yet, as I later learned, there was a kind of free-enterprise corruption going on in the Ninth right under my nose while I was working there.

I would have sworn no such thing existed. But it did.

The story came out after I had been transferred from the Ninth. We had an arresting-process officer named Robert Ellis. He was forty-one and was reported to have made one thousand arrests during his career. He was a tall man, with dark thinning hair and large, deep-set eyes. Something about his eyes and the curve of his mouth gave him a wiseacre look.

He had been transferred from the Seventeenth Precinct to the Ninth. The word was that he hadn't been liked very well in the Seventeenth. His job with us was to handle all the clerical details that have to be taken care of when an arrest is made. This freed the arresting officer from those duties and got him back on the street much more quickly.

For example, I would make an arrest and bring in my prisoner. I would give all the details to Ellis, and he would type up the various forms that had to be made out and filed. He was very good at his job, and I was back on the street in no time.

I never had any run-in with Ellis. I did my

job, and he did his. I didn't particularly like him or dislike him. That was all there was to it.

My relationship with Ellis was so routine that it came as a great surprise to me when I learned he had turned in five fellow officers in the Ninth on corruption charges. This happened right after I had been transferred out of the precinct, in December 1975. But the actions that led to the charges must have taken place while I was there. I had been on occasional patrols with some of the men charged, though none of them were regular partners of mine. Still, I had known them. But I had had no suspicion of what they were doing. It simply shows that you can be right in the middle of things and yet have no idea of what is really going on.

This, apparently, is what happened: Ellis, in handling the arrest details connected with his paperwork, noticed that some figures didn't add up. He spotted differences between the amounts of money supposedly taken in drug-related arrests and the amounts on vouchers turned in to the Department.

He decided that some of the green must be sticking to the fingers of arresting officers. He watched the pattern that was developing until he felt certain about what was going on. Then he went to his commanding officer. And his commander hustled him right over to the Internal Affairs Division at Police Headquarters.

Internal Affairs had the job of finding out about corruption and seeing that the Department ran straight. The first thing they did when Ellis went to them was to check his record out carefully. It was all clear. Internal Affairs concluded he had had no personal, vengeful reason to come to them. So they gave Ellis a tape recorder to be worn under his clothing. Then they told him to suggest to the suspected officers that he was interested in joining in their corrupt activities.

As the result of Ellis's activities, five of his fellow officers were arrested and convicted. A sixth was cleared of charges.

The worst case dealt with a twenty-two-year-old heroin dealer named Louis Pagan and the fifteen-year-old girl with whom he was living in a tenement at 709 East Sixth Street. Pagan had been arrested four times. Each time, the charges had been thrown out, the judge in each case having found that the arresting officers had acted illegally.

Pagan and his girl friend testified at the trials of the officers that the officers had gone through their apartment twice, stolen a total of fifteen thousand dollars from them—and roughed them up in the process.

Ellis contended that the lives of honest cops in the Ninth had been endangered by the activities of the dishonest ones. The dishonest cop's actions, he said, only lead to contempt and distrust of all members of the force. Ellis added that when a dishonest cop takes money to protect a crook—and later arrests the man he's taken the money from—he is going against "the street rules," by which "pimps, prostitutes, and drug dealers live."

"These guys cut it both ways," he said. "According to the street rules, if you take their money, you don't lock them up."

The activities of this small band of corrupt cops had been so outrageous that members of the community had filed a lawsuit against the Department. This was about the time Ellis began his undercover work. The suit accused

Matthew Smith, one of the officers later convicted and sentenced to prison, and the Department as his employer. The charges were false arrest, destruction of property, and harassment. The suit was dropped after the officers Ellis named were arrested and prosecuted.

In reporting his fellow officers, Ellis broke with one of the oldest traditions of the Department. This was the unwritten "code of silence" that held one officer must never inform or testify against another. So strong was this old tradition, that one officer ran his finger across his throat while Ellis was testifying—a clear threat to Ellis for breaking the code.

Yet that "code of silence" had been one of the main targets of the Knapp Commission. The Commission had held that, if the honest cop remains silent about his dishonest brother, he harms himself and the entire force.

That hurts all of us. Those of us who are trying to do a real job want the people to feel that we are on their side. We would like to have the kind of respect that Reddy and Glover had. But you can't have that kind of respect if all the street-wise guys know that some of you are on the take.

I suppose the reason I didn't know what was going on in the Ninth is that I keep pretty much to myself. I can be responsible for my own actions and stay out of trouble. But I can't be responsible for someone else.

Take a situation like this: You are on radio-car patrol with another cop from the precinct whom you don't know very well. He says to you: "Stop a minute. I'm going into this store to get a pack of cigarettes." He leaves, and you sit in the patrol car and wait for him. You don't know what he's doing. If he's on the take, if he's shaking somebody down, you may get in trouble just because you were with him.

This is one reason there are differing views in the Department about one-man patrol cars. There are two ways of looking at it.

If you are on patrol by yourself, you don't have any help, any backup, if you run into trouble. On the other hand, if you are patrolling by yourself, you can't be held responsible for what someone else may be doing.

That is one reason some of the men in the Department favor the one-man patrol-car idea. They feel that, if you happen to be working with an officer whose corrupt activities are uncovered, the Department is going to wonder about you, too. You were his partner, weren't you? So there is always the chance you can go right on downhill with him.

11

The Seventeenth

When I was transferred from the Ninth Precinct to the Seventeenth, in December 1975, I went from one extreme to the other. I went from one of the city's worst slum areas—a precinct that had the highest crime rate in the city—to the place where the rich and the diplomats lived.

The Seventeenth covers the heart of the wealthy East Side. The United Nations is there. Headquarters of various foreign missions to the United Nations are located along Second and Third Avenues all the way from the United Nations Plaza in the Forties up into the wealthy Fifties and Sixties.

In the Ninth, I had seen crime at its worst—crime on a scale I wouldn't have believed until I went there. In the Seventeenth, I saw an entirely different type of crime. It was no longer the dog-eat-dog crime of the Ninth, where in desperation the poor rip off the poor. Here, in the Seventeenth, the wealth of the region brings in criminals from outside the area the way blood in the water draws sharks.

Hoodlums come to the Seventeenth from all sections of the city. From Harlem. From the South Bronx. From the Lower East Side. The large banks, the best hotels, the big businesses in the area act like magnets. Thieves flock in from everywhere like cannibals drawn to a feast.

Bank robberies are frequent. They present a big problem. Take a regular working day, Monday through Friday. Say it's sometime between the hours of 9 A.M. and 3 P.M. You get a call: Code 10–11, First National City Bank. That means there's a bank robbery in progress. And you can be practically certain in those hours that it's the real thing. You turn on your lights and siren and go as fast as you can.

The trouble is that you can't go very fast. The traffic in these streets is just unbelievable. Unless you are lucky enough to be quite close to the scene when the call comes in, you'll never get there in time.

There are the Thirty-sixth-Street midtown tunnel to Queens and the Fifty-ninth-Street bridge to Queens. From about eight in the morning until seven-thirty at night, you meet the most impossible kind of traffic jams caused by cars coming into the city or cars trying to get out. And on the cross streets there's nothing but bumper-to-bumper traffic.

If you are anywhere near the tunnel or the bridge when a 10–11 comes in for a crime in progress at Fiftieth Street, it's almost certain that you'll get there ten or fifteen minutes too late. I don't understand people. They hear your siren, they see the lights flashing on the top of the police car—and then they don't make any effort to move over and give you room. They just sit there.

What can you do? Scream at them? Yell: "Can't you see these lights going? Can't you hear the siren?"

They just lower their car windows, stare at you blankly, and ask, "What did you say?"

Sometimes, the only way you can get around some of these idiots is to drive up on the sidewalk.

Pedestrians are almost as bad. The worst time is from shortly after eleven o'clock in the morning until about two in the afternoon. Those are the hours when some of the workers in large office buildings in the area go out to lunch. They're all in a hurry, and their minds must be wandering. We've got the lights on and the siren going—and they'll still keep crossing the street right in front of us. It's unbelievable. It's as if they don't give a damn.

The result is that it is very hard to catch criminals in this area. When you are fighting traffic roadblocks and mobs of people on foot, everything favors the criminal. He can pull off his job and get away before we can possibly get there. So everybody gets robbed.

The closest I've come to real action in the Seventeenth came on a Tuesday after I had signed out. I was working the midnight-to-eight shift that day, and I had just gone off duty when the eight-to-four crew that took over got a 10–11

90

call. The report was that a holdup was in progress in a drugstore at Fifty-fifth Street and First Avenue.

The team that had just taken over happened to be close enough to get there fast. As soon as they got within a couple of blocks of the scene, they turned off the siren and lights so that they could roll up quietly. They got out of the police car and looked into the drugstore. At first, they couldn't see a thing. Apparently, the holdup man who was looting the store was somewhere out of sight in the back.

The two officers split up. One guarded the front of the store, while the other slipped along an alley toward the rear. From his place behind the store, this second officer heard the owner begging the robber, "Please don't shoot me. Please don't shoot me."

The man was terrified, naturally enough. He kept begging for his life. All the time, the robber was stuffing all the drugs and money he could lay his hands on into a big shopping bag. Then he ordered the panic-stricken drugstore owner to keep quiet and not raise an alarm when he left.

As he came out, the two policemen were waiting for him, covering the entrance of the store from either side. The robber had his hand on the butt of what looked like a machine gun or a sawed-off shotgun. The barrel was hidden in the shopping bag.

"We're police! Drop it and put your hands up!" the officers called to him.

They both had their guns out, ready to fire. The robber must have known he had no chance. But, for some crazy reason, he made a motion as if to draw his gun from the shopping bag. You can't take chances in a situation like that. The officers both fired, and the man was killed on the spot.

Later, when the shopping bag was examined, it was discovered that he hadn't even had a real gun. All he had had was a toy gun. But the butt, which had been sticking out of the shopping bag—the only thing the officers could see —had looked like the real thing. They had had to fire.

I have described this case at some length as an example of the kind of crimes you have to combat in the Seventeenth. It's an area where you have some two million people coming in and out, going to work every day. It's a transient area. You don't have any close-knit neighborhoods as in the Ninth, depressed and miserable though they are. So you have less chance of getting information. With criminals coming in from all different sections of the city, there is little chance that anyone can give you a tip as to the identity of the robber in any one case.

The result is that these out-of-the-district goons work all kinds of rackets, and it's very hard to catch them. Some wealthy apartment dwellers go away for the weekend—and come back to find that their apartments have been looted in their absence. A delivery boy will go into a building, supposedly to deliver a package, and he will walk out with a purse he has snatched from a terrified old lady. There are all kinds of crimes like these in the Seventeenth.

One of our problems with coping with crime in the precinct is that so much of our time is taken up standing on post; we must be what I call butler-type cops. The presence of the United Nations headquarters in the area accounts for much of this. We have to stand guard at the UN. We have to protect the various missions, especially the Israeli mission. We have to keep demonstrations under control and sometimes guard against bomb threats. It takes up a lot of our time. In the Ninth, the only time we had to do this kind of duty was on Saturdays, when we protected the synagogues.

Standing on a fixed post for hours at a time is boring duty. It is not very productive as far as police work is concerned. Most of us think we shouldn't have to do this at all. You can't serve the public and catch criminals when you are put in front of a building to protect foreign diplomats.

This kind of duty sometimes causes another kind of upset. Some bosses will still expect you to make a lot of arrests. But how can you, when you're just standing there like a uniformed butler unable to leave your post?

That's one of the worst drawbacks of the job in the Seventeenth, but you have to get used to it and not let it bother you. What's the use? It's just part of the system. It's something you can't change and that you have to do. And I don't care what job you have, there's bound to be something about it you won't like. I know that, and I don't let things like this worry me.

94

12

Summing Up

I have tried to describe here the day-to-day life of a young policeman in New York City. My experiences, I think, are fairly typical of those of thousands who have joined the force as rookies —and then learned what it is like on the street.

One thing a rookie quickly finds out is that the policeman is a jack-of-all-trades. This is, of course, especially true in poverty-stricken districts like the Ninth. If there is a family dispute, we are almost certain to be called. We try to keep the husband and wife from killing each other. We act like lawyers in the case, questioning first one, then the other, to find out what has caused the trouble. Then we try to act as marriage counselors, to get the couple calmed down and on friendly terms—for the time being, at least.

Whenever there is any kind of trouble in a tenement, the police get called. The police are expected to take care of everything. Say the plumbing has broken down. Do the tenants call the landlord? No, they call the police. Perhaps they have learned from past experience that the landlord isn't going to do anything for them—so they call us. And we have to go in and see what we can do as plumbers.

Most persons on the outside don't think of the police doing such things. But these experiences, one soon finds, are routine on the job. They are not, of course, our main job. That is to deal with crime.

In this, there is sometimes danger. I have had to draw my gun many times, though I have never had to shoot. And often, there is boredom. I have had my share of standing guard on a fixed post for hours at a time in all kinds of weather.

I have seen crime at its worst in the Ninth—

and crime that victimizes the wealthy in the Seventeenth. I'll never forget fellow officers who were killed: Reddy and Glover.

After I have said all that, it remains true that, for me, there are many good things about the job. I am happy being a policeman. That is what I always wanted to be. It is what I still want to be.

When I look back, I think that I have been very fortunate. I began as a Puerto Rican kid who couldn't speak a word of English and who was suddenly dumped down in a tough section of the West Side. Now I am soon going to get a college degree—and Dina is getting her master's from John Jay College. Neither of us could have done that without some of the benefits and opportunities the Department provides.

I think it must surprise the living daylights out of my parents to think of my having a college degree. When I was growing up, I was always roaming the streets and playing with my friends. I wasn't the intellectual type. I wasn't "into" books.

My parents wanted to see me graduate from high school and get a good, secure job of some kind. My sisters were very bright girls, though they didn't have the money to finish college. But me? My parents, I'm sure, never thought of me as college material. And they were right. I never would have been except for a special program the Department started.

This is what is known as the College Accelerated Program for Police. It was set up in 1973 and is sponsored by the New York Institute of Technology. Instructors come to the precincts and teach courses there. It costs much less for a policeman to further his education this way than it would to go to college. The fact that I am a veteran helps too; I get additional benefits.

There are a lot of other advantages in being on the force. For example, I am in the military reserves and the Department grants me thirty days' military leave a year with pay. Many times, in private industry, you would be docked for the time you lost from your regular job while putting in your reserve training.

You get twenty days' vacation the first three years you are on the force. After that, you get twenty-seven days, nearly a month. You have unlimited sick leave. But, of course, if you take advantage of this and misuse it, you will be checked on. Taking too much sick leave doesn't look good on your record. But if you are truly ill and need it, it's there.

Then there is the pension system. We have a very good pension setup, and we share with the city the cost of paying into it. After you've been on the force, say, six or seven years, you'll have contributed some $3,500 toward your pension. Then, if you need to borrow money for some emergency, you can go to the Pension Bureau and borrow up to 75 per cent of the money you have personally put in. The loan will be paid back by automatic deductions from your pay-check. You don't even see the money, and so it is an easy and painless way to borrow if you have to. After twenty years' service, you can retire with a pension. Of course, your pension will be less than if you stayed on the job longer.

The Patrolmen's Benevolent Association will pay your drug bills if they amount to more than twenty-five dollars a year. If you become very ill and have to have costly prescriptions, you fill out a form and send the PBA the bills. They will then pay you back. It is a valuable protection.

These are just some of the advantages of being a policeman. But they aren't the real reason you join the force and stay with it. Dina and

I get a great satisfaction out of helping people. Like the time Pawelko and I saved the life of the man who had been stabbed. Or the time I helped a mother find her lost child. That gave me great satisfaction—just seeing her happy again.

The mother had been shopping along Fourteenth Street. She had her four-year-old son with her. There are a number of bargain stores along Fourteenth Street, and the sidewalks become crowded at times. The mother was looking for bargains, and when she turned around, her son was gone. He was lost. She became hysterical.

Since she was Hispanic, I spoke to her in Spanish. I tried to calm her down and assure her we would find her son for her. We did. We sent out a description of the boy, and in a few minutes, we found him. There was a pet shop several doors down the street in the other direction from the way the mother had been walking. The boy was there, staring at the dogs and other animals in the window.

It was a simple thing, but I got a lot of pleasure out of seeing the mother's happiness when she put her arms around her little son and hugged him to her.

Some of the worst times, on the other hand, are when someone dies suddenly. A police officer is always assigned to the case until the body is removed. It's one of the saddest parts of the job. You stand there helpless while a man's wife, daughters, or sons break down in tears. There's nothing you can do or say to help them. You just feel terrible.

For every tragic scene like that, however, there is usually one of another kind that makes up for it. One of the best things about the job is the surprises. You never know what is going to happen next.

I got a telephone call from Dina one afternoon, asking me to meet her in court. She had made an arrest on her way to work that morning, and she said, "Carlos, maybe you'd better meet me in court, because this guy's going to be awfully mad at me when he wakes up."

Here is what had happened:

It was a bitterly cold, windy winter morning. Dina got on a bus at 7 A.M. to go to her precinct. At the time, all you had to do was show your shield, and you rode free on the buses and the subways. Since then, the city has taken this privilege away from us, and I think that was a very short-sighted action. Under the free-ride system, policemen rode the buses and subways a lot—and that meant added protection on the lines. As it is now, most policemen use their cars. For example, Dina drives me to my station house and then goes on to her own.

At the time this happened, they hadn't yet changed the system. So Dina boarded a bus at Twenty-third Street to go to her station house on Thirty-fifth. She showed her shield and took a seat. Then she became aware that one of the passengers—a man who was obviously drunk—was annoying a young woman. The girl, seeing that Dina was a cop, came and sat beside her for protection.

This didn't stop the drunk.

"He came up to me and started jabbing his fingers at my eyes," Dina says. "I said to myself, 'Why me, God?' But I had to do something, so I got up and said to him, 'Mister, you'd better be nice and go and sit down.'

"With that, he called me every name in the

book. I have never heard curse words put together so well in my life.

"I was getting mad. I grabbed him by the collar, rammed my knee into his back, and told the driver to stop the bus. I shoved him down the steps and slammed him up against a wall. There was a meter maid passing by, and I asked her to call the precinct to send a car. I kept him covered and jammed up against the wall until they came.

"We put him in a cell to sober up and wait for a hearing. In the meantime, we found out who he was. He was an actor who had had some good roles in two major motion pictures, *Serpico* and *The Sting*."

After Dina learned who her prisoner was, she called me to meet her in court because she thought, once the actor sobered up and found out he had been manhandled by a tiny blonde, he would be a raving lunatic.

It turned out he was just the opposite. At the hearing, Dina told the judge, "You know, Your Honor, I have worked for the Department of Corrections, I've worked in jails, and I have to tell you that I have never heard the language out of anyone's mouth like that I heard out of this man's."

The judge fined the actor fifty dollars. He was really embarrassed and ashamed of himself. He came up to Dina, and instead of being angry, he couldn't apologize enough.

"I was never so mad in my life," Dina says. "I didn't want any part of it. I said, 'Just get away from me, vanish.' I didn't want an apology. I just wanted to get him out of my sight and get lost."

Of course, it isn't every day that you arrest a character like that, nor every day that you save a man's life. There are, as I have said, bad times, dangerous times, plain boring times.

But I don't care what job you have, there will always be some things about it that you don't like—things you have to put up with. The grass, they say, always looks greener on the other side. But it isn't always so.

A lot of others must feel the same way I do. Some ten thousand people took the last examination the department gave, in 1973. And I understand there's a waiting list of some seven thousand who have qualified. They are on the hiring list, waiting their turn if the city's finances ever improve so that the Department can begin hiring again.

As for me, the satisfactions of a policeman's life outweigh the disadvantages. I have done what I have wanted to do ever since I was a boy. I have reached my goal. And along the way, I found Dina. Could any man ask for more?

Fred Cook is a graduate of Rutgers University. A newspaper reporter of vast experience as well as a free-lance writer, Mr. Cook has forty books to his credit. He has written numerous magazine articles for *Reader's Digest, American Heritage,* and the New York *Times Magazine.* He has won Page One awards from the New York Newspaper Guild three different years, and received the Sidney Hillman Award in 1961.